The Wolf in Sheep's Clothing

and other Aesop's Fables

Compiled by Vic Parker

Miles

First published in 2013 by Miles Kelly Publishing Ltd

Harding's Barn, Bardfield End Green, Thaxted, Essex, CM6 3PX, UK

2 4 6 8 10 9 7 5 3 1

Publishing Director Belinda Gallagher
Creative Director Jo Cowan
Editorial Director Rosie McGuire
Designer Joe Jones
Production Manager Elizabeth Collins
Reprographics Stephan Davis, Jennifer Hunt, Thom Allaway

ISBN 978-1-84810-987-2

Printed in China

British Library Cataloguing-in-Publication Data
A catalogue record for this book is available from the British Library

ACKNOWLEDGMENTS
The publishers would like to thank the following artists who have contributed to this book:
Cover: Tamsin Hinrichsen at Advocate Art
Advocate Art: Natalie Hinrichsen, Tamsin Hinrichsen
The Bright Agency: Marcin Piwowarski
Frank Endersby
Marco Furlotti
Jan Lewis (decorative frames)

Made with paper from a sustainable forest

www.mileskelly.net   info@mileskelly.net

www.factsforprojects.com

Contents

The Fox
and the
Crow

A **crow once spied** a piece of cheese
on the ground. She swooped
down and picked it up in her beak.
Then she flew to a nearby tree,
where she settled on a branch.

A fox was lurking in some bushes
nearby and saw what she had done.
He licked his lips at the thought of
the delicious cheese.

The fox strolled up to the foot
of the tree and cried, "Mistress Crow,

how well you look
today, how glossy
your feathers, how bright
your eyes. I'm sure your voice
must be just as beautiful. Sing for me,
please, so I can tell everyone that
you are the Queen of Birds."
The crow was thrilled by
these words. She lifted her
head and began to
caw – and the cheese
fell to the ground.

The fox pounced on it at once, snapping it up in his jaws. "That was all I wanted," he said. "In exchange for your cheese I will give you a piece of advice – when people pay you compliments, they may not be telling the truth."

Do not trust flatterers.

The Vain Crow

Long ago, the great god Jupiter ruled over the Earth. One day, he was looking down over all creation when he saw that the birds were arguing and squabbling amongst themselves.

'This will not do,' thought Jupiter. 'There must be a way that they can keep order amongst themselves.'

Jupiter thought hard, and finally came up with an idea. He announced that he intended to appoint a king of the birds, to rule over

them and keep control. The god named a day on which all the birds were to appear before his throne, when he would select the most beautiful to be their ruler.

The birds were hugely excited – all of them wished to be chosen. Wanting to look their best, they hurried off to the banks of a stream, where they busied themselves in bathing and preening. The crow was also there, but he realized that, with his ugly feathers, he would

have little
chance. So he waited
until the others had
gone, and then picked
up the brightest of the
feathers they had dropped, and stuck them all
over his own body. When he had finished, he
looked at his reflection in the water – he was
very pleased with his handiwork.

When the day came, the birds assembled
before Jupiter. One bird caught the eye of the
great god because of its bright plumage – the

9

crow. But just as Jupiter was about to make him king, the other birds turned on the crow, stripped him of his feathers, and exposed him for the unremarkable bird that he really was.

Dressing up does not make you a better, more worthy person.

The Tortoise
and the
Birds

Once upon a time, there was a tortoise who wanted to find somewhere new to live. He wasn't exactly sure where – all he knew was that he was fed up where he was and wanted a change. He thought that if the eagle picked him up, she would be able to carry him high up in the sky from where he could look down and see all the land below. Then he would be able to decide where he wanted to live.

So he asked the eagle if she would help him, and promised her a rich reward for her trouble.

The eagle agreed, and seizing the tortoise by the shell with her talons, she soared aloft.

As the eagle flew over the landscape, they met a crow, who said to the eagle, "Tortoise is good for eating."

"Ah yes," said the eagle in reply. "But the shell is much too tough."

"Those rocks would crack the shell," was the crow's answer, nodding down below.

And the eagle, taking the hint, let the tortoise fall down onto the sharp rocks. Then the two birds made a meal of him.

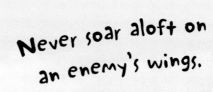

Never soar aloft on
an enemy's wings.

13

The Fox Without a Tail

Once upon a time, a sly fox caught his tail in a trap. He struggled and struggled to get free, and as he twisted and turned he broke loose – but his tail was left behind.

The fox was mightily relieved. However, his relief soon turned to embarrassment about no longer having a tail. He felt so ashamed, he did not want to show himself in public. But he was determined to put a bold face upon his misfortune, and summoned all the foxes to a meeting.

When everyone had assembled, the fox showed them that he was tailless. Then he proposed that all foxes should do away with their tails. He pointed out how inconvenient a tail was when they were pursued by dogs. The fox reminded them that it was in the way when they wanted to sit down. He said that there was no point in carrying around something so useless.

"That is all very well," said one of the older foxes, "but I do not think you would have asked us to do away with our beautiful brushes if you had not lost yours."

Do not trust interested advice.

The Wolf in Sheep's Clothing

There was once a wolf who kept trying to steal sheep from a flock. However, the shepherd and sheepdogs were very watchful and always chased him away. But the wolf did not give up. He hung around, waiting for a chance.

His chance came one day when he found a sheepskin that had been cast aside. He put it over his coat and tied it around him, so he was

quite disguised. Then he strolled among the sheep – none of them noticed anything strange. In fact, the lamb of the sheep whose skin the wolf was wearing began to follow the wolf.

Leading the lamb away from the flock, the wolf made a meal of her. And for some time afterwards, he succeeded in deceiving the sheep, the shepherd and the sheepdogs, and enjoying hearty meals.

Appearances can be deceptive.

The Milkmaid and her Pail

Once upon a time, a milkmaid was walking to market, carrying her milk in a pail on her head. She began to plan what she would do with the money she would get for the milk.

"I think I'll buy some chickens from Farmer Brown," she said, "and they will lay eggs each morning, which I can sell to the pastor's wife. With the money that I get from the eggs, I'll buy myself a new dress and

a new hat, and when I go to market, all the young men will come up and speak to me! Polly Shaw will be jealous... but I don't care. I shall just look at her and toss my head like this."

As she spoke she tossed her head back, the pail fell off, and all the milk was spilled.

Do not count your chickens before they are hatched.

Belling the Cat

Long ago, a group of mice were terrorized by a cat. Every day, the cat made their life a misery by hiding roundabout, spying on their holes and waiting for them to come out.

The mice held a meeting to discuss how they could outwit the cat. Some said this, and some said that, but at last a young mouse got up and said he had a proposal to put forward.

"You will all
agree," he said,
"that our danger
lies in the sly way in
which the enemy lurks about,
waiting for us. If we could receive
some signal of her approach, we could easily
escape. I therefore propose that we get a small
bell and attach it round the neck of the cat.
Then we will always know when she is about."

This proposal met with a lot of clapping, until
an old mouse got up and said, "But who is going
to volunteer to tie the bell on the cat?"

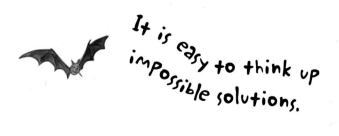

It is easy to think up
impossible solutions.

The Deer
and the
Lion

A **deer was once being chased** by hounds.
As he grew tired, he looked around
desperately for a hiding place. At last,
the deer saw a cave where he
hoped he would be safe from
his pursuers. He dashed inside,
panting furiously.

Unfortunately, a lion
lived in the cave and the
deer was completely at
his mercy.

Realizing his fate the deer cried, "I am saved from the power of the dogs only to fall into the clutches of a lion."

Out of the frying pan into the fire.

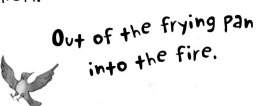

The Fox and the Cat

There was once a fox and a cat who were discussing what was the best way to escape from enemies. The fox was boasting about how he always outwitted his enemies.

"I have a whole bag of tricks," the fox said, "which contains a hundred different ways of escaping."

"Well, I have only one method of escape," said the cat, "but I can generally manage with that."

At that very moment the fox and the cat heard the cry of hounds. They looked at each other in horror, then the cat scampered up a tree

and hid herself in the thick, leafy branches.

"This is my plan of escape," she said to the fox. "What are you going to do?"

The fox thought first of one way, then of another... And while he was wondering which would be best to choose, the hounds got nearer and nearer... The fox was so caught up in confusion that he did nothing at all. The hounds caught him and he was killed by the huntsmen.

Better one safe way than a hundred that you cannot be sure of.

The Eagle, the Cat and the Wild Pig

In the middle of a forest there was an enormous old tree. At the very top, an eagle built her nest. In a hollow halfway down the trunk, a cat settled in with her family. And in the tangle of roots at the bottom lived a pig and her little piglets.

All the creatures might have got on very well if it hadn't been for the cunning of the cat. Climbing up to the eagle's nest she said to the eagle, "You and I are in the greatest possible danger. That dreadful creature the pig, who is

always grubbing away at the foot of the tree, means to uproot it, so that she may gobble up both your family and mine." At this, the eagle was driven almost out of her mind with terror.

Then the cat climbed down the tree, and said to the pig, "I must warn you against that dreadful bird, the eagle. She is just waiting for her chance to swoop down and carry off one of your little piglets to feed her brood with." The cat succeeded in scaring the pig just as much as the eagle.

Then she returned to her hole in the trunk, from which, pretending to be afraid, she never came out by day. Only by night did she creep out unseen to find food for her kittens.

The eagle, meanwhile, was afraid to stir from her nest, and the pig dared not leave her home among the roots. In time, both they and their

families perished of hunger, and the cat and her family had the tree all to themselves.

Those who stir up suspicion and hatred are not to be trusted.

29

The Grasshopper and the Owl

There was once an owl who lived in a hollow tree. She fed by night and slept by day, as all owls do. But whenever she was trying to sleep, her slumbers were greatly disturbed by the chirping of a grasshopper, who had made his home on a log beneath the tree.

The owl tossed and turned and tried everything she could think of to block out the grasshopper's singing and get to sleep. But nothing was any good. The owl begged the grasshopper repeatedly to have some consideration and stop chirping, but the grasshopper, if anything, only sang louder.

At last the owl could stand it no longer, and was determined to rid herself of the pest by means of a trick. She said to the grasshopper, in the most pleasant way she could, "As I cannot sleep for your song, which is as sweet as harp music, I have a mind to taste some nectar. Won't you come in and join me?"

The grasshopper was flattered by the praise of his song, and his mouth watered at the mention of the delicious drink, so he said he would be

delighted. No sooner had he got inside the hollow where the owl was waiting than she pounced upon him and ate him up.

Do not let flattery throw you off your guard against an enemy.

The Bat, the Bramble and the Seagull

A **bat, a bramble, and a seagull** once fancied themselves as businessmen and dreamed of being rich. They went into partnership and decided to go on a trading voyage together. The bat borrowed some money for the trip, the bramble brought a stock of clothes, and the seagull gathered an amount of lead, and so they set out.

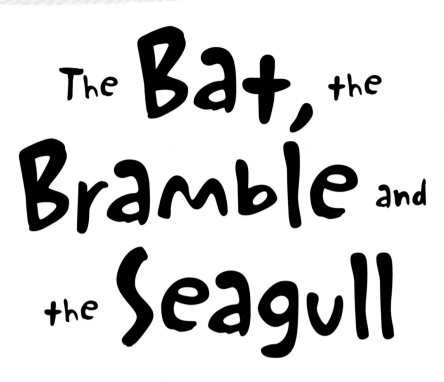

They loaded a ship with their cargo and sailed away. By and by they sailed into a great storm. The wind buffeted the boat and the waves battered it until great holes appeared. The boat, with all the cargo, sank to the bottom of the sea. Luckily, the three travelers managed to stay afloat and were washed onto the shore.

Ever since then, the seagull flies to and fro over the sea, and every now and then dives below the surface, looking for the lead he's lost. The bat is so afraid of meeting the money-lenders he borrowed from that he hides away by day and only comes out at night. And the bramble catches hold of the clothes of everyone

who passes by, hoping some day to recognize
and recover its lost garments.

People care more about recovering
what they have lost than acquiring
what they lack.

The Sly Lion

There was once a lion who came across a fat bull feeding in a meadow. The lion watched and waited, his mouth watering as he thought of the feast he could make. But he dared not attack for he was afraid of the bull's sharp horns.

However, the lion grew more and more hungry. He knew that if he tried to pounce, he wouldn't be successful, so he resorted to cunning instead. He went up to the bull and said, "I cannot help but admire your magnificent figure. What a fine head. What powerful shoulders. But, my friend, what in the world makes you wear those ugly horns? You must find them awkward. Believe me, you would do much better without them."

The bull was foolish enough to be swayed by this flattery, and the next day he had his horns cut off. Of course then he had lost his means of defence – and fell easy prey to the lion.

Beware of flatterers – they often want something.

The Cat and the Mice

Once there was a house that was overrun with mice. A cat heard of this, and said to herself, "That's the place for me," and off she went to live there. Every day, the cat caught the mice one by one and ate them.

After a week, the mice had lost so many of their friends they could stand it no longer. They decided to stay in their holes and not come out until the cat gave up and went away.

'Hmm,' thought the cat. 'The only thing to do is to trick them out.' So she came up with a plan.

The cat climbed up the wall then grasped a peg with her hind legs, lowering her body until she was hanging upside down. She pretended to be dead. The cat thought the mice would be fooled and come out.

By and by, a mouse peeped out and saw her hanging there. But it wasn't taken in.

"Aha!" it cried. "You're very clever, but you won't catch us anywhere near you."

Don't be deceived by the innocent ways of those whom you have once found to be dangerous.